I0725996

The

Challenge

Anthony Clive

Published by

Dayglo Books Ltd, Nottingham, UK

www.dayglobooks.co.uk

0010-14-0103-25

Cover artwork & illustrations by
www.valentineart.co.uk

Typeset in Opendyslexic
by Abelardo Gonzales (2013)

Printed by IngramSpark

Distributed by Filament Publishing Ltd, Croydon

The Challenge

Chapter 1   Two Young Men

Peter Salt dug his heels in and felt the familiar thrill as Belle broke into a gallop. Her hooves threw up small clouds of dust from the dry earth beside the river.

Peter crouched forward, his head low over his mare's mane. At last he pulled on the reins and Belle slowed down, first to a canter and then to a trot.

Peter turned his horse to face the way they had come and began to canter back towards the city walls. As he neared the gate he saw another horseman coming towards him.

From the awkward way the newcomer rode he recognised the poet and writer, Henry Martley.

Although Henry did not share Peter's love of horses and sports, he was his closest friend.

Peter gave a wave and once more kicked Belle into a gallop. It was not only that he was keen to meet Henry, there was also an urge to show off his skill to his friend.

"Well, Henry, what was it your father wanted you for?" Peter asked, when they drew level.

"There's going to be a contest to decide which country owns the Saints Islands and you've been picked to be Voravia's champion!"

"What – me?" Peter pulled up sharply.

"Why me? There must be far better candidates."

"There probably are. But I'm afraid you're the one who's been chosen."

"What sort of contest? And what's so important about these islands anyway?"

"The islands lie just off our coast, guarding the entrance to Newport harbour. My father says they have political value to Voravia. It would be a disaster if they fell into an enemy's hands."

"And I suppose the enemy you're talking about is Sloronia?" Peter asked.

"It is," Henry nodded. "There has been a dispute between Voravia and Sloronia over which country owns the islands for almost a hundred years – since 1463 to be precise.

"There are seven islands in a group and they're all named after saints," Henry continued.

"So that's why they're called the Saints Islands?"

"Exactly right, Peter!" Henry smiled.

"The islands are all very small," he continued. "No one lives on six of them. But the largest one, called St Anne's, has a village with a church. That church is important. Whoever owns the church, owns all the islands."

"So the church really matters."

"Yes, it does," Henry agreed. "Wars have almost broken out over the islands in the past. At last, good sense has triumphed.

"Now, there is to be a contest between a champion from each nation to decide who owns them. That is why this contest is so important."

Chapter 2   The Contestants

"I see." Peter paused. "You haven't told me yet what the contest consists of."

"Riding, running, swimming, fencing and boxing."

"Swimming! I can't swim a stroke. No, Henry, you must choose someone else."

"You don't have to win them all, just three. You're a fine horseman. I'm sure you'd excel at any form of fighting and you must stand a good chance in the running. Besides, Sloronia's man may not be able to swim either.

"Anyway, I've been sent to summon you to the Grand Council to be formally appointed as Voravia's champion."

"But there must be someone else who could do it," Peter protested.

Henry shrugged and shook his head.

"I'm too young," Peter insisted. Surely there's someone older and better?"

"In theory there is. But neither the first nor the second choice can take part."

"Who are they?"

"The first choice was Sir Lucian Astley."

"Yes, he'd be everybody's first choice," Peter agreed. "He's not only a great sportsman, he's got wonderful horses, the best in all Voravia.

"I don't know if he can swim, but I'm sure he'd

give a good account of himself in the boxing and running. He's an aristocrat. He's bound to be good at fencing."

"Yes," Henry nodded, "he would be."

"Well then, why not choose Sir Lucian?"

"Sir Lucian rode into Newport from his estates this morning and can you believe it? As he was getting off his horse, he trod on a bucket, slipped and broke his leg."

"You're joking?"

"Afraid not."

"So who was the second choice?"

"The Earl of Blagdon. He'd probably do almost as well as Sir Lucian, better in the boxing probably. He's a hard, tough fighter. And that's the problem.

"We've learnt that he fights for money and

that is not allowed. If you get money for fighting, that makes you a professional, and professionals are not allowed to compete.

"The champions are supposed to represent all that is noble. Fighting for money, or any kind of reward, is banned."

"All the same, Henry, surely your father could find someone better than me?"

"Peter we've no time. The contest is set for Monday."

"Oh, no!"

"So, my friend, although you don't have a drop of noble blood in your veins, you're our last hope. It will be all right to come as you are. We've no time to lose. So come along."

Henry turned his horse towards the city and,

reluctantly, Peter followed.

The two friends reached the city gate. They spoke to the guard, gave their names and were allowed to pass into Voravia's small capital.

Chapter 3   The Queen's Regents

Most Voravians, unless they were from the highest of the nobility, would have been very anxious, even terrified, about appearing before the queen in her council.

But Peter knew Voravia's queen, the Princess Lucy, well.

Five years earlier, when he was twelve and she eleven, they had studied together. Lucy's father, King Charles, had insisted his daughter learn the new sciences that were sweeping across Europe.

Peter's father, William, was the town's

apothecary. He was skilled in science and medicine. He was able to cure many diseases.

The king had selected William to teach his daughter science.

The king also decided Princess Lucy would learn better if she had a companion. He chose Peter to be her fellow student. So Peter and the princess studied together and became firm friends.

The tragic death of King Charles had meant that the princess would, when she reached twenty-one, be crowned queen. But until that time, she had two regents who, together, ruled in her place.

Now that he was seventeen, Peter was not sure if Princess Lucy was still just his friend. Was she something more?

He would have been even more certain that he was falling in love with her if it had not been for

Lucy's sixteen-year-old lady-in-waiting, Elspeth.

Lucy, probably because of her position, had a rather distant air to her. She could appear quite cold. Not so the lovely Elspeth, with her mop of red-gold curls, dimpled smile and curvy figure.

She was just the sort of girl any boy would boast about. And she took no trouble to hide her admiration for Peter.

Peter knew he should consult Henry. It was not because Henry was a year older. No, it was that a poet would understand, better than most, matters of the heart.

The trouble was, Peter suspected Henry was in love with Lucy and, as a poet, his love would be of an especially passionate sort.

It was all so complicated.

They handed their horses to Jack Farthing, the head stableman at the royal stables, and presented themselves to the guard at the palace gate.

A footman in fine silks was waiting for them. He quickly gave instructions.

"Master Martley, Master Salt, you are to follow me. You are expected."

He led them through a great empty hall, up a short flight of steps and into a panelled corridor. The footman tapped at a door and opened it.

"Master Henry Martley and Master Peter Salt," he announced.

It was not the great chamber Peter had expected. Nor was there any sign of the Grand Council.

The room was cosy. It was hung with bright

tapestries. Peter could imagine that in the winter
a bright fire would crackle in the grate.

Princess Lucy rose from behind her desk. She
was very simply dressed. Her fair hair was held in
place by a pale blue silk band.

She was wearing a soft silk dress in an off-
white colour over her slim, boyish figure. It was tied
at the waist with a simple, pale blue cord.

The only fancy touches to her dress were the
lace frills at the wrists and throat.

The two other people in the room were her
regents.

The Earl of Bardsey was Voravia's treasurer.
He was a stout, elderly gentleman in a fine doublet.
He looked to be a man who lived comfortably.

The other man was Voravia's great military

commander, Sir Walter Martley.

Sir Walter was Henry's father. Peter knew he had risen from the humblest of backgrounds.

Sir Walter was dressed in the simple leathers of a soldier, with a sword at his waist. Over his left eye was a leather patch.

Peter had never dared ask Henry what the eye patch hid and whether Sir Walter took it off at night.

"Peter, how are you?" Lucy asked. "How often I remember those happy days when we were scholars together! And now look at me, worn down with care.

"If only Papa were still alive, I could be as jolly as I was then. If it were not for Sir Walter and dear old Bardsey here, I don't know what I should do."

"My lady, you would govern with as much good sense as any other European king," the gallant Earl of Bardsley responded.

Lucy did not contradict him.

"My lady," Henry began, "I have explained the situation we find ourselves in to Peter and that he is our last hope. I think he will agree to be Voravia's champion."

"My lady, gentlemen, I fear I will let down not only you, but our nation," Peter burst in. "I'm sure Sloronia will choose someone who is better than me at everything. And anyway I can't swim."

Now that the task was presented to him he felt a terrible fear of not being up to it.

"Peter, all we can ask is for you to try," the princess replied with a smile.

"I know you will do your very best. You don't need to assure us. No nation could have such a determined champion.

"Even if Sloronia field a giant like Goliath –
well, we all know how that battle ended. Goliath
didn't win. Will you help us?" Lucy begged her friend.

How could he refuse? Surely this was love?

Chapter 4   My Lady's Picture

Henry turned to his friend.

"Peter, I really do think you should do this for Voravia. If you refuse you'll regret it for the rest of your life. I think you could win. Indeed I might place a small bet on your success, if I can find some decent odds."

Sir Walter looked sternly at his son.

"Henry, I trust you have not started betting. Your mother has often warned you against gambling and drinking and going with low women."

"Where will the contest take place?" Peter asked, changing the subject. "What are the rules?"

"We have until this evening to give our response," Sir Walter replied. "I take it you agree to represent us?"

Peter nodded. What else could he do?

"In that case, our ambassador will send back a message telling them to prepare."

There was no backing out now.

"The contest will take place in Sloronia," Sir Walter continued. "It will be held at the town of Trois, which is quite convenient. We'll go by sea. That will be the quickest way."

"I've never been to sea." Here was a new anxiety for Peter.

"Oh don't worry. Modern ships are very safe."

Peter was more concerned with sea-sickness than safety.

"You'll need a second," Sir Walter went on. "Someone to help you and look after your interests. Is there anyone you would trust?"

"Oh, it must be Henry!" Peter replied quickly.

Sir Walter looked unsure.

"Of course, I'm flattered you should choose my son, but please don't do so just to please the two of us. Perhaps you should find someone more – shall we say – sporting?"

"I shall have need of a trainer, of course, Sir Walter. I'm sure you can come up with a soldier who will train my body.

"But I will need someone to look after my mind, and there is no one I'd trust half as much as Henry."

Peter turned to his friend. "Will you do this for me?"

"Most certainly. If I've a few florins riding on your success you will not find a more loyal second."

"Henry," Sir Walter scolded, half joking, "if your mother learns of the way you appear to be willing to ignore her advice in this matter, she may jump to the conclusion that you are going with low women."

"Father, would I? A monk couldn't be more pure."

"Your mother will be most pleased to hear it," said Sir Walter, although Peter thought he detected a certain amount of disbelief in the old soldier's tone.

"Now," Sir Walter continued, "I think, Peter, you should go and explain matters to your parents. Then let us meet at the stables to select the best horse there. I believe we still have some of Sir Lucian's horses."

Peter and Henry had not gone far from the gate to the royal stables when they met a pedlar.

The man thrust a piece of cheap paper at them. It was very poorly printed and showed a girl sitting side-saddle on a horse. She was as naked as the day she was born. Below the picture were the words: 'My Lady . . .'

"You can have any name here," the man said, "and I will give her what colour hair you like. Or, sir, you can have this one. Lots of folk choose it. It's very popular."

He showed them a second identical picture. This time the title read: 'My Lady Elspef'. The artist had given her red hair, red nipples and a smudge of red lower down. Elspeth was the toast of Newport.

He should, Peter thought, have been outraged.
After all, she was his girl – well, almost his girl. Yet
in a way he was rather proud to think she was the
cause of such desire.

For a moment he was tempted, then said no to
the offer. Henry bought one. He tucked it into his
purse. What would his mother think!

Peter feared his parents would not welcome
the news that he had, under pressure, agreed to
champion Lucy on behalf of Voravia. He was not to
be surprised.

"Peter, how could you agree?" his mother
Abigail cried. "Sloronia has had months to find
a champion. You'll be beaten in everything and I'm
terrified what will happen to you in the boxing."

Abigail, as all mothers do, could only see her
son as the little boy he once was. She could not bear

to think of him risking all the dangers the contest

would throw at him.

"Mother, what choice did I have?"

His father, William, was more practical. "You're

right. You had no choice. You must make the best of

matters.

"You'll lose the swimming. You should win the

running. If you have a good horse you stand a good

chance at riding. As for the fencing, well I'm no

expert, but Henry tells me you're a fine swordsman.

"It may not come down to the boxing. I hope it

doesn't. I've only been to one prize-fight. It was

a terrible spectacle. They were professional fighters

and neither would give way. They fought until one

was unable to stand. We must hope you don't have

to go through that."

Chapter 5   Emir

Peter left his home no less worried than he had been when he arrived there. He was glad to have Henry at his side as they walked up to the stables.

If Peter had thought he would have to explain matters when he got there, he need not have worried.

News that he would be Voravia's champion in the contest between Voravia and Sloronia, had reached the stable yard long before he did.

Jack Farthing, the head stableman, was in a fever of excitement.

"Sir Lucian is with his Emir. That is the fastest horse in all Voravia. He has said you may ride him."

"I must see Belle first," Peter said. He picked an apple from the barrel and went to Belle's stall.

When he was weighing up how much he loved Lucy or Elspeth he left out Belle. But in many ways, she was his true love.

King Charles had given Belle to him very soon after he and Lucy had started studying together. She was as fast a mare as any young man could wish for.

Long before he was at her stall Belle was leaning over the door and whinnying her pleasure.

Peter gave her the apple. As she munched it, he buried his head in that hollow below her ear. He breathed in her lovely scent and ran his fingers through her mane.

"I'll always be loyal to you," he whispered.

He came out into the bright sunshine of the yard and found every stable lad pressing forward. They were thrilled to see someone they knew given a chance to ride the pick of Sir Lucian's famous horses.

Sir Lucian was with his Arab racehorse, Emir. Sir Lucian was leaning on a crutch.

"Peter, I congratulate you." He offered his hand. Peter suspected that behind his kind words was a terrible regret that he had not been chosen.

"Lucian, I'm only our second – no, actually, our third choice. You were the obvious one. It's dreadful about your injury."

"Oh, it's typical. Go through a war without a scratch, then cripple myself on a bucket."

Peter thought the man looked close to tears.

Sir Lucian pulled himself together and hobbled to one side. Peter took his first look at Emir.

He was magnificent. His head was narrow with almost wild eyes and small delicate ears, and his body was all muscle.

Peter found his excitement growing at the prospect of riding such an animal, bred for one thing only – speed.

The lads put the harness and saddle on Emir. All the while Sir Lucian was intent on giving Peter useful bits of advice about his horse's behaviour, his soft mouth and the tactics best suited to Emir's stamina. Peter listened intently.

He could not avoid noticing a short, muscular man standing by the well, chewing a straw.

Peter judged him to be about twenty-eight.
Although he was dressed very plainly in dark, worn
leather, he had the confident air of an aristocrat. He
looked like a fighter.

When all was ready, Peter was lifted into
Emir's saddle by two lads, who were delighted to be
part of things.

Sir Lucian was put up into a saddle. So was
Jack Farthing and two stable lads. Then the little
procession of mounted horsemen made its way down
the valley to the gallops along the river.

Peter should not have been nervous. Emir
was as fast a horse as most people would ever
experience. He knew how to ride. Yet his mouth was
quite dry.

They passed through the Lower Gate and soon
found themselves on the stretch of beaten earth that

ran beside the river, where earlier that morning he had been riding. He had ridden here so often with Lucy and Elspeth, all his memories were happy ones, yet now he felt almost sad.

"Let's go." Sir Lucian dug his heels in.

Peter turned Emir, gave him a slight nudge and they were off.

Although Sir Lucian had quite a lead, Emir sailed past him and now they were out on their own.

Peter leant forward. He gripped the reins but determined to put no pressure on Emir's soft mouth.

When he was on Belle he found she hardly needed to be guided. A very slight transfer of his weight would let her know which direction she should take.

He tried this with Emir, but the method didn't

work. He supposed horse and rider needed to learn each other's ways over many months.

He reined in and Emir slowed to a canter. As he did so Peter pulled gently on his left rein. The horse began to turn, but it was a slow, awkward turn. Then they were facing back down the gallops.

Peter gave Emir a sharp kick and they were off once more, racing back towards the others, who seemed a long way off. Peter and Emir had covered the mile at a breathtaking speed.

Halfway back he met Sir Lucian who had slowed to a walk. Peter dropped to a canter and then pulled up. Once again he tried to turn Emir and once again the turn seemed to take forever. Emir was blowing quite hard.

"What am I doing wrong? I can't turn him."

Sir Lucian didn't answer for a few moments. Then he said, "I saw you turn at the far end. That seemed fast enough. Some of these pure-bred Arabs do take a bit of getting used to.

"To be honest, I've never put Emir through a race of that length. Still, he's fast. You should have a big enough lead to be able to afford a slight delay on the turn."

Peter turned Emir once more and they trotted back to Jack and his lads.

When they arrived there was much chatter about Emir's speed. They all agreed he was as near to flying as was possible.

The party returned to the stables. Peter swung himself from the saddle and went round to give Emir a stroke.

He touched the horse's soft muzzle. Emir backed away. It was that little sign of drawing back from him that finally decided Peter.

"Lucian," he said, "few men with so fast and valuable a horse would lend him to someone else. You are truly generous. But I shall ride my Belle. She is not so quick perhaps, but she is a real stayer and she will turn on a pin point.

"She and I know each other so well. She will suit my riding style better."

"But, Peter . . ." Jack Farthing and several lads began to protest that he was turning down the finest horse they had ever seen.

"He's right," Sir Lucian interrupted them. "I have two old horses back at the stables. I'd entrust my life to them. Emir is faster, much faster, but do you know, I am sure that if I were to race for Voravia over four miles, I would choose one of them.

"When something really matters, like this up-coming race, you need to have a good friend with you. I know Peter and his Belle. They're as fine a team as we could wish for.

"Belle came from my stable, so she'll always be an Astley mare at heart. It will be a privilege to have her race for Voravia."

Peter looked across at Sir Lucian Astley. The man was not particularly bright. Henry could be quite cruel about him only having one topic of conversation – horses – but he had as generous and kind a nature as you could wish for.

"Now, we had better go and tell Belle she has an important date. She'll carry not only her friend but the hopes of the nation." Sir Lucian led the way towards Belle's box.

"Who was that fellow in the yard, by the well?" Peter asked Sir Lucian.

"The Earl of Blagdon. He's the son of a duke. I think he's annoyed he was not chosen. If I had been selected it wouldn't have been quite as bad for him. At least I come from one of the old families.

"But he will see the decision to appoint you champion as just one more example of the way power and fame is being passed to commoners – what King Charles used to refer to as his new men."

Peter listened closely.

"Now, Peter, please believe me," Sir Lucian continued, "I bear you no grudge at all.

"It's true most of the upper classes don't like the way men like Sir Walter and now the Lady Elspeth and you are coming forward. But I see it as a chance to refresh the breeding stock. I mean, just look how much better our horses are with the introduction of these Arab newcomers."

"Lucian, you are the most loyal citizen Lucy could wish for," Peter replied. "And I confess the idea of breeding with Elspeth had crossed my mind. Now I shall see it in a whole new light."

"I'm sure you're not alone there," Sir Lucian chuckled. "Most of the young men of Newport probably have the same idea."

After Lucian had left, Peter turned to his beloved mare.

"Belle, Emir was quick, but I chose you. I may not be highly bred, but not even the greatest aristocrat in the horse world could find fault in your breeding."

He found he was blinking back his tears.

Belle looked him back with her steady, dark eyes and gave a tiny snort.

"I knew you'd be faithful. I never doubted it," was what she said.

Chapter 6   Sergeant Ben Watts

"Master Peter Salt?"

"Yes, that's me."

"I'm Ben Watts. Sergeant Ben Watts."

The large, jolly-looking man thrust out a great paw of a hand and gripped Peter's.

"Sir Walter has sent me to prepare you for this here contest. Now, young Salt, there is no time to waste. I hear there's to be fencing – that will be with them French rapiers – and running and boxing."

"And swimming." Peter added.

"Aye, well don't look at me to teach you to swim. If the good Lord had meant us to swim he'd have given us fins.

"Now, as I said, we ain't got much time. Master Henry, I'd be obliged if you would go to the armourer to get two rapiers, two daggers and two face guards.

"Now about the riding, Sir Walter tells me as how you've got one of Sir Lucian Astley's horses."

"Ben, I shall ride my Belle. I had a try on Sir Lucian's Arab racehorse, and a wonderfully fast horse he is, but I will be more confident on my old friend."

"Well it's not what most would do. But I'm no horseman. That's for you to decide. I don't suppose you need much training there, though you can be sure your opponent will have a fine horse.

"We're going to tackle the running first, Peter.

What's the distance? How far is this here race?"

"A half-mile. It's a long way. I don't think I've ever run that far. I am told it will be the first event."

"The order of events could be important. The last one is bound to be the boxing. By the time you get to that, it could come down to the fittest man, not the strongest."

Sergeant Ben looked around the yard.

"Jack, who is the fastest boy here?"

Jack Farthing pointed to a boy about Peter's age, but taller and slimmer.

"You, lad, come over here. Jack says you can run," Sergeant Ben called out.

"Aye, Sergeant."

"What's your name, lad?"

"Tom, Tom Phelps, Sergeant."

"Well, Tom, I am sure you know we're all depending on Peter here to win the contest. I am putting you in charge of preparing him for the running. Can you do that?"

The stable lad looked horrified.

"Tom, I really do need your help," Peter told him. "Look, I'm no aristocrat. I'm just like you. Come on, I need someone to race against."

Tom nodded. "All right. I'll do my best."

"Good!" Sergeant Ben Watts was pleased. "Right then, the pair of you, get off down to the gallops and then, Tom, you make sure Peter runs his half-mile.

"Meanwhile, I'll bring some horses down so you can ride back."

Peter went across to Tom and clapped him around the shoulders.

"From now on, Tom, you're in charge. Let's go."

Tom took off his sandals.

"First thing, Peter, is to get your feet tougher. You'll run a lot faster barefoot, but if you're not used to it they'll bruise and maybe cut. Try to go without sandals until the race."

"Thank you, Tom. You've already taught me something. I'd never have thought of that."

Chapter 7   Training

Peter removed his shoes and they ran down to the Lower Gate, skipping over the little streams of waste water that crossed the path and drained the city.

This was downhill and Peter felt quite fresh by the time they reached the gallops for the second time that day. His feet hurt at first, but now they seemed to be almost numb.

"If it's a half-mile, we must take it steady," Tom advised. "Run within ourselves. You run on my shoulder."

They set off. If Peter had expected a slow start he was quickly put right. Even running as Tom put it 'within himself' he went at a fast pace.

After they had gone less than half way Peter had to stop. He was gasping for breath. Tom turned a worried face to him.

"Give me a minute or two. I haven't run for ages," Peter gasped. They waited until he had recovered.

"I say we run at half that speed to the end," Peter suggested. "I must finish or it won't count."

They set off again at a brisk pace and this time Peter managed to keep running until they arrived at the half-mile marker.

They turned and, as there was no sign of Sergeant Ben with the horses, Tom began to run back.

Peter gritted his teeth and ran with him. He was determined not to drop to a walk.

When they were about half way they saw Sergeant Ben arrive with two horses on a leading rein.

Sergeant Ben halted the horses and waited at the start of the gallops. Tom and Peter would have to run all the way back to him.

Despite all his efforts, Peter was falling behind. When they were nearly there, Tom turned his head.

"Try to keep up with me," he told Peter, over his shoulder. Then he lengthened his stride and began to speed up.

Peter found his legs just would not respond. He barely managed to reach Sergeant Ben. He collapsed at the sergeant's feet.

"How did he do, Tom?"

"Very well, Sergeant. If that was his first run,
he'll soon be quick."

"Good. Now tomorrow I want the pair of you
down here early. And I mean early. I'll be here and
I don't like to be kept waiting."

They mounted and rode back to the stables.
Henry was waiting with the midday meal, the fencing
weapons and a neat little man in a tight-fitting
doublet and hose.

Peter climbed off his horse and collapsed onto
a bench. He wolfed down his bread and ham, and
drank half a jug of water.

"This is Monsieur Patrice," Henry introduced
the little man.

"He's the fencing master. I met him at the
armourers. I thought he could teach you some tricks."

Henry helped Peter into his face guard and then handed him the dagger and the rapier. The sword had a button on its point to avoid injury.

"The dagger is only to be used to parry – that is to say, ward off a blow," Monsieur Patrice explained. "You must not use it on your opponent. The hits must be made with the rapier."

Peter took up his position opposite the fencing master. His legs felt shaky from the running, and even his arms did not feel as strong as they would normally be.

As Sergeant Ben Watts had said, this competition would be as much about stamina as skill – who lasted out the better.

Monsieur Patrice proved a clever coach. He could have impressed the bystanders with a display of his skill, but he did not.

Instead, he toned down his fencing to suit Peter's level of skill.

After a few minutes he stepped back and pulled off his face guard.

"Peter, you are new to this sport. Your problem is, you fence like a soldier trying to be a sportsman.

"I think Sloronia will choose a young nobleman, someone you would have no difficulty beating on the field of battle with a sword, but who will have learnt the art of fencing.

"I just do not have the time to bring you up to the necessary level of skill. If you try to use the traditional fencing moves, he will win."

"Well, what am I to do?" Peter was devastated. "I shall lose the swimming. My running is not good enough in spite of Tom's kind remarks. I've turned down the fastest horse in Voravia and although I will thrash any young noble in the boxing, the matter could be settled before then."

The Frenchman thought for a moment. Then he replaced his face guard.

"Peter, fight as you would on the field of battle. But remember, only hits with the point of the rapier count. You must surprise and confuse your opponent. Now try."

Peter's approach was completely different. At the end of ten minutes, Monsieur Patrice pulled back once more and removed his face guard. He was sweating and grinning.

"Well done, Peter. It's a long time since I have fought like that.

"The referee may have something to say about your method, but you have history on your side. Two hundred years ago, fencing was not the upper-class sport it has become now. Then, it was much more like your style of fighting. Where will the match take place?"

Henry answered. "At Trois, in Sloronia. So we will have the crowd against us. The riding and running will take place in the Guild Square. It will be four circuits running and eight riding. Then the fencing and boxing will be held in what they call the arena.

Monsieur Patrice may have been a French fencing master to the nobility, but he knew the power of the common people when they were aroused.

"This is what I hope," he told Peter. "There will be a mob of Sloronian people shouting and baying.

Although their man may fight strictly within the rules of fencing, the crowd will want to see a proper fight. And you can give them one. Let us hope the referee will want to please the crowd."

That made Peter feel a little better. He went across to Belle's stable. He quietly saddled her up and led her through the yard.

"Shall you want some company?" Jack Farthing's tone was one of an anxious father.

"I'll be fine, thanks," Peter smiled, grateful for Jack Farthing's kindness. "I just thought I'd put my girl through her paces." Peter gave Belle a friendly slap on her rump.

The ride, that late afternoon along the gallops, was so unlike that on Emir.

Belle wasn't as fast – he couldn't expect her

to be – but he felt they were part of each other, so close was their understanding of each other.

Now he knew the race was to take place on a circuit with tight turns, he was even more certain he'd made the right choice.

He tried riding Belle with sharp turns.

Henry had learnt they would run with his left shoulder towards the centre of the square, so he began to school Belle to take sharp turns in this direction.

Surely, Sloronia would never find a horse and rider to match them. In this event, at least, he felt he stood a chance.

It was with a much more cheerful heart that he rubbed Belle down, gave her an extra portion of oats and a kiss on her soft nose.

As he left the yard he was told that they would sail on the Monday tide – the day after tomorrow. This was not an official announcement but, judging by the speed and accuracy of all the other news the stables managed to obtain, Peter assumed it to be correct.

The party would include his running mate, Tom, to manage the horses.

Chapter 8   You Idle Man

Peter was up early. He dressed, but left off his shoes. He snatched some breakfast and was about to set off for the gallops and his appointment with Tom and Sergeant Ben when his mother appeared, looking messy and half asleep.

"Peter, it's Sunday. You will want to attend Mass at St Mary's."

Peter had forgotten what day it was. Abigail would make sure he carried out his religious duties. The urgent need to prepare himself for the contest had driven everything else from his mind.

"Mother, I'll be back long before Mass, but I must go now. Sergeant Watts will never forgive my being late. Mother, if I can win the riding, the running and the fencing, there'll be no need of the boxing."

Abigail turned a worried face to her son.

"Oh, don't even mention the boxing, Peter. I dread to think of it."

Peter unbolted the door to the shop and set off through the awakening city to the Lower Gate. He arrived to find Sergeant Ben and Tom waiting.

The guards were surprised to have to open the gate so early. A quick explanation from Sergeant Ben Watts and they were let through – and all those not on guard duty dressed hurriedly and followed them out, intent on watching the training.

"Right, lads, remember, it's a half-mile race,

not a sprint. You . . ." he turned to one of the guards who was standing watching. "I want you to set off quick and I want you, Salt, to take no notice of him. Take it steady and you'll run him down."

The startled soldier began to object, but Sergeant Ben quelled him with a curt: "You heard what I said. Now jump to it."

The man set off.

"Run, I said, not dawdle, you idle man!" Sergeant Ben yelled and the soldier quickened his pace.

After he had gone about a hundred yards Sergeant Ben sent Peter and Tom off. Peter shot away. "No, slow down," Tom called. "Run at my pace."

Peter slowed and allowed Tom to catch him up. They moved at a steady speed and yet Peter noticed

that with every step they began to narrow the gap
between them and the leader.

"He's slowing already," Tom called, "he'll be
walking soon."

They passed the pace-setter before they had
reached halfway and now Peter began to struggle to
keep up with Tom.

When they had only a hundred yards to go,
Tom turned his head and gasped: "Now run as fast as
you can. If you're level when you get this far, you
must break him now."

Peter made a great effort. His legs seemed
made of lead, his lungs were aching, but he managed
to increase his speed and arrived at the half-mile
post just ahead of Tom. He fell to the ground,
panting for breath.

Tom sat down beside him.

"Well done! You're a fine runner! You ran me to a standstill."

Peter looked up and smiled. He could see that Tom still seemed to have plenty of running left in him and had probably allowed him to win. All the same, he felt he had improved on the previous day's run.

"Now we'll take it nice and easy, just jog back to the sergeant."

Peter staggered to his feet. "Tom, you're as hard a taskmaster as Sergeant Ben Watts. If I win, it will be thanks to you."

Tom's idea of a jog was something not much slower than a run. Peter was completely exhausted by the time they arrived back where Sergeant Ben

Watts was awaiting them with a bucket of water.

They were surprised to find that the Earl of Blagdon was waiting close by. He was seated on a fine horse, but wearing the same coarse leather clothes as on the previous day. He rode across to them and spoke to Peter.

"I see you will be running barefoot. That should give you an advantage."

"That was Tom's idea." Peter indicated his companion. "I just hope I can toughen up my feet in time."

"Have you given any thought to the boxing?" the Earl of Blagdon asked.

"I'm rather trusting that the man Sloronia has chosen will have had less experience of using his fists than me."

"Care for a short bout?" the Earl enquired. "We could put a few florins on it?"

The man looked as tough as any prize-fighter. He would probably give Peter a very hard time.

Besides, the prospect of going against the Sloronian champion, after taking a battering two days before from the Earl of Blagdon, was absurd.

Even so, Peter did not want to appear frightened by the Earl. He chose an excuse.

"No, but thanks anyway. I promised my parents I'd be back for Mass."

The Earl gave a toss of his head.

"Well, if you fancy a little practice or watching how a prize-fight goes, come and find me. I'll be at the yard behind The Two Cocks inn. Drop by. You might learn a thing or two."

He turned his horse and trotted back towards the town gates.

Tom came up, with Sergeant Ben Watts.

"Well done, boys!" Sergeant Ben told them. "Unless Sloronia has chosen Tom's brother, we should have that event in our purse.

"Just remember, Peter, the speed you ran at this morning. That's your pace over the race. Can you remember that?"

Sergeant Ben was looking highly pleased with Peter's progress.

"Where is The Two Cocks inn?" Peter asked.

If anyone would know the location of a tavern it would be an old soldier like Sergeant Ben Watts.

"The Two Cocks? That's in a very rough neighbourhood. It's in Lazetto, just as you start down the hill. Not a place a gentleman like you would want to go drinking."

Peter nodded.

If he went, he would wear his sword.

"The referees for the contest have been chosen," Tom announced. "They will be the two English ambassadors. I heard it last night."

Once again, the stable yard was the first to know.

Chapter 9   With God's Blessing

Peter returned to his home and peeled off his shirt. It was soaked with sweat. He went out into the yard and plunged his hands into the water barrel, scooping it over his body. The shock of the cold water made him flinch.

He went up to his room and shaved himself. Then he put on a clean white shirt and his Sunday-best hose and doublet.

He made a very unsuccessful effort to tame his curls and came down to meet his parents as they were preparing to leave for Mass.

In spite of Tom's instructions, he felt he could not go barefoot to church with the family.

All over Newport the church bells were ringing to summon the people to pray.

St Mary's church was a fine building with beautiful paintings on the walls inside. They showed scenes from the Bible.

When it came to the sermon, Father Jerome gathered his congregation around one of the paintings.

This was the part of the service the people looked forward to. Children were pushed to the front where they could have the best view.

Father Jerome had a long stick in his hand and he pointed to a small figure at the top left of the picture.

"There is Moses. You can always recognise him with his beard and his yellow gown. He is on top of the mountain and look . . . here is God giving him the Ten Commandments on two stone tablets.

"Now look here," and he moved his stick towards the middle of the picture. "Here we have Moses again – see his yellow robe – he is carrying the two stone tablets under his arm."

The yellow-robed figure, now rather larger, could be seen making his way down between the rocks, clutching the tablets.

Peter could not help but be impressed by the man's strength. The tablets were quite large and made of stone, yet the old man was able to manage them as if they were written on parchment.

"Now down here we have what Moses found when he got back to the camp of the Israelites."

The priest moved the pointer again.

"What does he find? No sooner is his back turned than they have set up an altar to an idol. It's a golden bull. Here is Moses." Now Moses was a life-sized figure. "He is angry."

The people pressed forward to get a closer look at the picture, and Father Jerome allowed them a few minutes whilst parents explained to their children what was happening.

Once Father Jerome had judged that everyone understood the famous story, he spoke for a few minutes, drawing a lesson for his people from the events that had taken place all those years ago.

The service concluded with a surprise.

"Brothers and sisters, this week, Peter Salt will, on behalf of our royal lady, Princess Lucy, pit his strength against the champion of Sloronia. Let us ask God's blessing on a child of our parish. May he have the courage to be a worthy champion of our nation and be granted victory."

There was a resounding "Amen" from the assembled company. Most of them had known the Salt family for many years.

When Peter and his parents emerged from the church, Peter was surrounded by well-wishers slapping him on the back and shaking his hand.

There were shouts of encouragement and advice, mostly concerning the need to knock the Sloronian out.

The midday meal at Peter's home was a quiet, sober affair. After it was over Peter decided to take a walk around the town, barefoot.

He would attend the prize-fight. He might pick up some tips.

He did not tell his parents, Abigail and William, of his plan. He was sure they would not approve.

He left, carrying his boots.

Chapter 10   The Two Cocks

The streets Peter padded through at the top of the town were deserted. Their respectable citizens were sitting quietly at home, some possibly even studying their Bibles as recommended by the church.

But, as soon as he turned off the main road and entered the narrow lane that ran steeply downhill into Lazetto, he was in a hurly-burly of activity.

The lane was of bare earth. Its sides sloped steeply to a central hollow carved by the rains.

It was full of household, animal and human filth. On either side, the foundations of the houses were exposed so that their doorways were well above the level of the street.

The buildings leaned towards each other at odd angles. They looked as if they might collapse at any minute.

The stink of sewage and rot filled his nostrils. Everyone was busy. It may have been Sunday, but the citizens of Lazetto had no time for rest.

He found The Two Cocks tavern with no difficulty. Above the door was the name of the landlord – Geoffrey Hardcastle.

In the street outside men were peeing against the tavern's wall.

A battered sign showed a picture of a pair of

fighting cocks, the one down on its back, the other about to slash it with the spurs fixed to its feet.

It was evident that The Two Cocks was much more than just a drinking den. Such noble sports as cock fighting, bear baiting, dog fighting and boxing also took place here.

Peter quickly put on his boots and pushed open the door nervously. It led into a passageway.

In the first room he was greeted by a roar of sound and a seething mass of men. He quickly closed the door.

He went down the passageway. He noticed some of the 'My Lady Elspef' posters tacked to the walls.

The door at the end opened into a yard.

There, behind the inn, was another building.

Peter went in. It was one huge space with raised stands all around the walls up to the roof. In the centre, at ground level, there was a stage area with sand on the floor. It was enclosed by a six-foot-high fence.

This was where the entertainment took place. People in the stands above would have a good view of the action below.

At the moment nothing was happening. The place was almost empty. The spectators had evidently gone out to refresh themselves and relieve themselves.

Peter took up a position towards the top of the stands at the back.

He noticed two men counting out coins. These, he thought, must be either the winnings from a bet, or the men were preparing for a new bet.

There was a shout and a surge of sporting men

burst in and packed themselves onto the stands.

Amongst the noisy mob was a group of well-dressed

young noblemen.

They elbowed their way to an enclosure at the

ringside. Then, from their midst, Peter saw the Earl

of Blagdon climb into the ring.

He was stripped to his breeches and his

knuckles were bound with linen tape. His muscular

body was covered in black hair.

At his arrival there were cheers from the

crowd – and several boos.

The Earl was accompanied by his second who

waved his scarf to the crowd.

Now a third man climbed into the ring. He was

wearing a long, shabby cloak, intended, no doubt, to

give him an air of authority. He carried a small drum, which he beat for silence.

"Geoffrey Hardcastle at your service, my lords!" he cried.

He was the landlord of the inn and the promoter of the fight. There was a roar of approval from the crowd.

"Gentlemen," he continued, "who dares challenge the Earl? A purse of no less than fifty florins has been put up by his friends. Come on, now, there must be some good sporting folk here."

Several names were shouted out and finally a huge, dark, nasty looking opponent was hustled from the crowd and into the ring.

"The brave challenger is Gypsy John Lee," the landlord bellowed, banging his drum.

He could hardly make himself heard above the noise of the crowd.

All around Peter bets were being placed.

Many of the spectators had had too much to drink and several fights broke out between them. Blows were being exchanged in the crowd before any had been thrown in the ring.

A little man followed the challenger into the ring to act as his second.

Another man joined them. He was the referee. He shook hands with the two fighters and then warned: "Now Gypsy John, you know the rules – no biting, no head-butting, no low punches and no swearing."

Gypsy John nodded.

The second carefully strapped Gypsy John's

hands, then both seconds took up their positions in opposite corners.

The referee called the two fighters to the centre. They stood there toe to toe. The referee stepped back and the fight began.

Gypsy John swung a wild blow at the Earl, who parried it with ease and smashed his fist into the other man's face.

Gypsy John took a step back and now the Earl tore into him, forcing him back against the boards and subjecting him to a flurry of powerful blows.

It was all over. Gypsy John fell to his knees and shook his head to acknowledge defeat. He climbed shakily from the ring.

The Earl of Blagdon removed the tape from his knuckles and rubbed them. He went across to his friends, who leant down to slap his back.

A strange hush fell across the room. The crushing defeat of the challenger had left a feeling that mixed awe with fear amongst the spectators.

The Earl looked slowly around the audience and then strode across to the landlord. He pointed up at Peter and whispered into the landlord's ear.

The landlord beat his drum and shouted.

"Gentlemen, we are indeed fortunate. We have here Voravia's champion, who will fight in two days' time against Sloronia's champion. Step forward, Peter Salt. Geoffrey Hardcastle at your service, sir."

All eyes were now on Peter. Panic seized him. He knew what would happen next.

Chapter 11   A Match

It was hopeless. Peter was grabbed by those closest to him. He pleaded, in vain, that he had to fight a far more important battle in Trois, but the drunken crowd would hear nothing of it.

After all, what did they know of the value of the little islands he would be fighting for?

He was dragged down to the ring. Well-wishers slapped him on the back as he passed them. A dozen arms hoisted him over the barrier that surrounded the pit and he dropped down onto the sand.

"Gentlemen!" cried the landlord, Geoffrey Hardcastle, banging his drum. "We have a match. The Earl of Blagdon against Peter Salt of Voravia.

"The Two Cocks has never before staged such an aristocratic bill. You'll tell your grandchildren you saw this famous fight.

"Now, a big reception for our nation's champion. Welcome my young sport. Ah, thank you, gentlemen."

The landlord made a bow to the gentlemen supporting the Earl.

"The purse has been increased to one hundred florins! One hundred florins! The greatest purse for the greatest fight!"

The next moment, a huge man with a smashed nose and a twitchy eye jumped into the ring beside Peter.

"You'll need a second, Salt. Bartholomew Smee, at your service."

"Bartholomew, this is a disaster. I'll be in no state to run, ride, fence, let alone box, if Blagdon deals with me like he did that poor fellow just now."

"Well then, your best hope is to win."

"Win! You must be joking! No, I reckon my best hope is to be beaten quickly."

"Now, Master Salt, you listen to me. The Earl has already had four fights. All right, they were quick ones, but he'll be more tired than he thinks. And his hands will be bruised.

"What you've got to do is box clever. Keep him moving. In boxing it's your legs that go first. Spare your fists. Don't hit his head – that's all bone. Hit him here." Smee pointed to his throat.

"It will hurt his breathing. It will worry him. His method is to counterpunch. You saw what happened just now. Don't rush at him. Let him come onto you. Try mocking him. Tease him. Get him angry, that will tire him more. The crowd will be with you."

All the while Smee was giving Peter these instructions, the crowd were shouting out and laying bets.

The Earl himself was lolling against the wooden walls of the ring, exchanging jokes with his friends.

"Now let's see to your bindings. No, first take your doublet off."

Peter kicked off his boots, unbuckled his sword and removed his doublet.

He looked around for someone he could hand his sword to while he fought. He chose the least dishonest looking man he could see in the crowd.

"You just teach that bully boy a lesson," the man said.

Bartholomew beckoned to the Earl of Blagdon's second to come across and witness the binding of Peter's fists.

He took two lengths of linen and wound them around Peter's fists so as to protect the knuckles.

At last, the landlord beat his drum for the bout to begin.

The referee stepped forward and drew a line with a rod across the filthy sand. Next he called the seconds to bring their men up to the line he had scratched in the sand.

Nervously, Peter approached the centre and his opponent.

Close up he could see how powerfully the Earl of Blagdon was built. Peter had never fought someone so much older than he was. Ten years of extra maturity had allowed the Earl to put on muscle and weight, particularly around the shoulders and upper arms.

Peter's only advantage lay in being taller and having a longer reach.

He must, as Bartholomew had said, keep his opponent at a distance. The tactic of wearing the Earl down was a good one, but Peter was very much aware that his own legs had done the morning run. It was quite possible they would give out first.

Peter stood with his left foot on the line. He held his left arm forward, with his right he prepared to parry the first blow.

His heart was pounding. His mouth was dry. He

felt red hot. All around, the people of Lazetto howled for blood.

The Earl did nothing. He was waiting for Peter to attack him. The fighters began to slowly circle each other.

Gradually the noise stopped. Peter made a cautious prod with his left hand and the Earl brushed it aside, then jabbed towards Peter's head.

The next moment Blagdon rushed him in a whirl of fists. Peter took a blow to his left temple and only avoided a second one by jumping aside.

The Earl spun round and Peter hit him hard just below the throat. Blagdon stopped just long enough for Peter to back away and know that he had hurt his opponent.

The Earl resumed his advance. Peter was

forced back towards the wooden sides of the ring.

Blagdon was trying to push him up against the boards.

Once again, the Earl launched a flurry of blows. Peter ducked the first, took the second above his right eye, but managed to slam his right fist into Blagdon's throat again.

Now it was Peter's turn to advance. He prodded at Blagdon with his greater reach. Twice he connected with his target. A dull red patch now showed where Peter's fists were starting to bruise the soft area round Blagdon's throat.

The Earl threw a blow. Peter parried it, but the next moment his mouth was hit by a fist that broke through his guard. Peter tasted blood.

The room was hot and both men were gasping for breath. They had been fighting now for four or five minutes. Although Peter's legs were starting to tire, he could see the Earl was slowing down too.

"Keep him moving," Bartholomew yelled.

Peter worked his way towards the centre. Every time the Earl tried to hit him, he slipped to the side and prodded hard with his left hand, using his reach to keep a distance between them. Another minute passed. The Earl was now beginning to look distressed.

"Come on, man, fight," Peter shouted, and beckoned his opponent towards him with his right hand whilst moving from side to side.

The crowd seemed to sense the fight was going against the Earl now. There were whistles and yells of abuse directed at him.

The Earl lowered his guard. He held both fists level with his chest and hurled himself at Peter.

Peter was ready for him. His left fist caught the Earl once more below the throat. Now, for the first time, he swung his right fist at the Earl's head and it smashed into the Earl's unprotected nose. The whole place rang with cheers.

Blagdon stopped. He stepped back. His nose was pouring with blood. Peter advanced carefully, but the Earl had had enough. He dropped one knee to the ground.

The referee stepped forward and pushed Peter away. "Set the timer!" he ordered.

The Earl slowly rose. He extended a hand.

"I'm offering you a draw," he said.

For a second Peter thought of turning down the offer. Good sense won. The Earl was hurt but not beaten.

With another fight two days away Peter agreed to the Earl's offer.

He took the Earl's hand. "I accept."

The cheers stopped as Peter went back to Bartholomew.

"They don't like it, Peter. They wanted you to thrash him. And now, no one knows what will happen to their bets."

"I decided I have a more important fight and, I tell you, I'm utterly exhausted."

Peter watched as the Earl of Blagdon climbed out of the ring, clutching his shattered nose.

Chapter 12   A Generous Gesture

A great wave of relief swept over Peter. He got his sword back and re-buckled it to his belt. Then he picked up the landlord's drum and beat it for silence.

"Friends and fellow citizens," he yelled. "On the dawn tide I sail to fight in Sloronia. I shall fight for our nation!" He paused and there were a few cheers.

"For our royal lady, the Princess Lucy!"

Now there were shouts and stamping of feet. He drew his sword and waved it in the air.

"And for Lazetto!"

The extravagant, showy gesture worked. The crowd's patriotism was fired up.

Cheers, shouts, stamping feet and whistles greeted him as if he were a king urging on his troops before battle.

By now Peter was swept along by the occasion. "And for my sweetheart, the Lady Elspeth!" he bellowed.

Now pandemonium broke out. It was mostly whistles, and some good-natured but very outspoken suggestions as to how he should show his love.

The landlord came across and handed Bartholomew Smee half the purse.

The landlord turned to Peter.

"Peter Salt, I don't remember seeing such

a stylish display. You should consider a career in the ring. You'll need a ring name. Now let me think. Yes, I have it – Stylish Salt, the gentleman fighter. That will pack the lads in. You'll always be more than welcome here at The Two Cocks. Lazetto loves a boy who can fight."

Peter refused his winnings.

"Take ten for yourself, Bartholomew, and split the rest with everyone here."

That wouldn't be easy, but Peter wanted to calm down the men who felt they had lost the chance to win on their bets.

Peter judged that Bartholomew Smee was a power in Lazetto and would manage the situation somehow.

The landlord banged his drum again and called

for order so that Stylish Salt's generosity could be announced. A further cheer greeted this.

Peter climbed out of the ring and began to push his way through the crowd. He was slapped on the back and offered hands to shake.

"Well fought, Peter! Pity you didn't finish him off." Jack Farthing from the royal stables was beaming all over his face. "I'll get them rude pictures of your girl taken down fast as you can say Lady Elspeth – not as how folk here don't fancy your lass."

Refusing offers of drinks, Peter forced his way into the street and turned for home.

In the street he came across the Earl with his party of friends. There was an awkward pause. For a dreadful moment Peter thought they would set upon him as a group, but then one of the Earl's friends stepped forward.

"That was a generous gesture," the man said, "sharing your purse. Here, take this florin as a reminder of a fine fight."

Under the circumstances it would have been stupid to cause offence, so Peter took it with a smile.

"I was lucky. Your man had had too many earlier contests." He put the coin in his purse.

"Good luck in Trois," the fellow wished him. "Some of us will ride over to cheer you on. We leave this evening with a string of horses. If we ride through the night we should be there in a couple of days, in time for the contest."

Peter would be leaving on the tide with the expectations of his nation on his shoulders.

But although his body was aching – from his battered face to his bruised feet – and his legs were shaking from exhaustion, his heart soared.

He knew he could win the running and the horse race. He would lose the swimming. He had a chance in the fencing, but if it came to the boxing, well, surely Sloronia would never field a fighter like Blagdon. He should win.

To find out what happens when Peter goes to

compete in Sloronia, look out for 'The Contest' –

Volume 2 of 'Voravia's Champion' – to be published in

our second catalogue.

Characters :

Peter Salt The person chosen as Voravia's champion

Belle Peter's horse

Henry Martley Peter's best friend

Sir Lucian Astley Young nobleman keen on horses

The Earl of Blagdon Young nobleman keen on boxing

Princess Lucy Uncrowned Queen of Voravia

William Salt Apothecary, father of Peter

Lady Elspeth Lady-in-waiting to Princess Lucy

Jack Farthing Head stableman at the royal stables

The Earl of Bardsey Treasurer and regent of
    Voravia

Sir Walter Martley Voravia's military commander and second regent. Henry Martley's father

Abigail Salt William's wife and Peter's mother

Emir Sir Lucian Astley's racehorse

Sergeant Ben Watts Old soldier, Peter's sports coach

Tom Phelps Stable lad, Peter's running mate

Monsieur Patrice Fencing master

Father Jerome Priest at St Mary's church

Geoffrey Hardcastle Landlord of The Two Cocks

Gypsy John Lee Fighter at The Two Cocks

Bartholomew Smee Drinker at The Two Cocks

Word meanings :

Apothecary – scientist, skilled in medicine, in the

days before modern science

Arab – fast racehorse

Armourer – person in charge of armour and weapons

Canter – speed of a horse, between trot and gallop

Circuit – route of a race

Dawdle – move slowly, waste time

Doublet or **Doublet and hose** – the fashionable dress

for men at the time

Florin – coin worth quite a lot of money

Gallop – fastest speed of a horse

Gallops – a place to ride horses at a gallop

Goliath – Bible giant killed by the young boy David

Half-mile – race distance equal to 800 metres

Israelites – people in the Bible story of Moses

Mare – female horse

Mass – church service

Muzzle – animal's nose

Panelled – lined with carved wood

Patriotism – loyalty to a country

Pedlar – street salesman

Purse – money bet on the outcome of a race or fight

Rapier – thin, narrow sword used in fencing

Regent – wise person who rules in place of a young
royal until they are old enough

Second – person who helps a contestant in a race or
fight

Stall – place for a horse in a stable

Tablets – stone slabs with carvings on them

Tapestries – thick, colourful rugs hung on the
walls inside old castles

Treasurer – person in charge of money

Trot – Speed of a horse, faster than walking

Whinnying – noise made by a horse

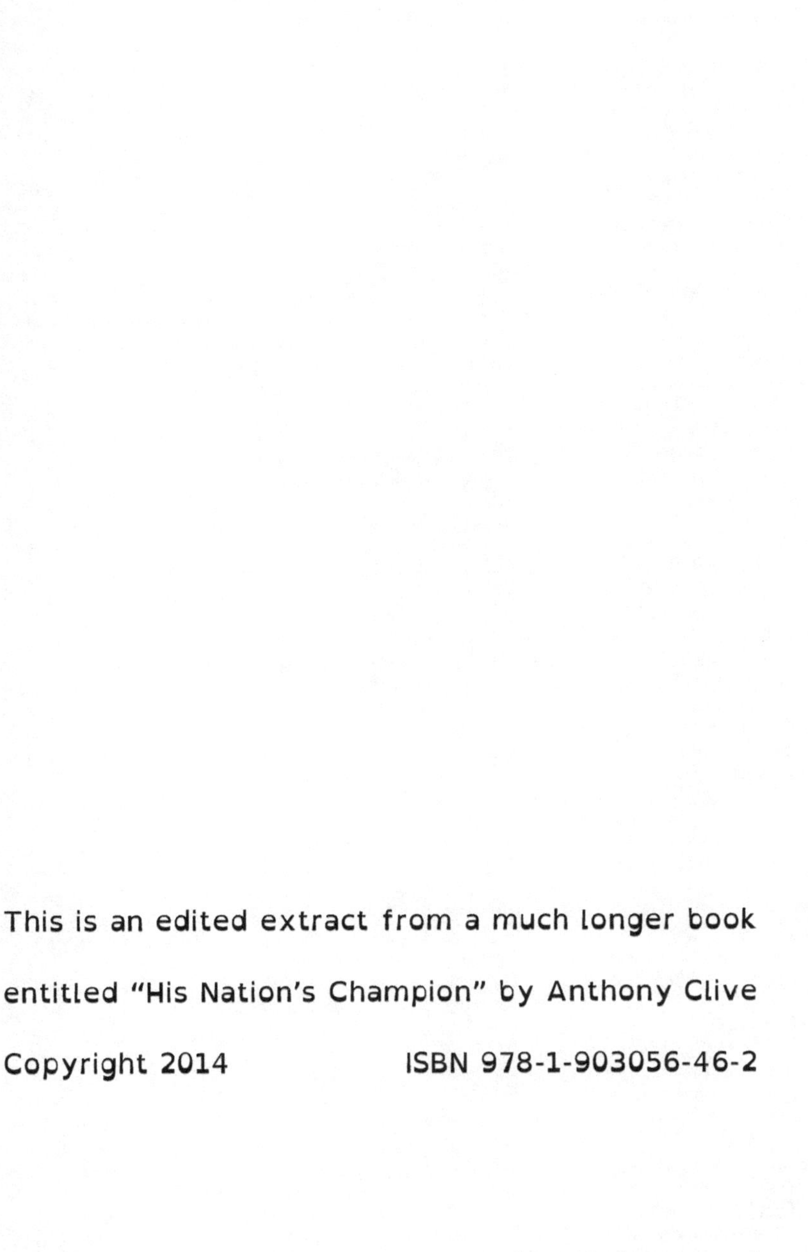

This is an edited extract from a much longer book

entitled "His Nation's Champion" by Anthony Clive

Copyright 2014   ISBN 978-1-903056-46-2